MARINI • SMOLDEREN • POP

NEGATIVE EXPOSURE™

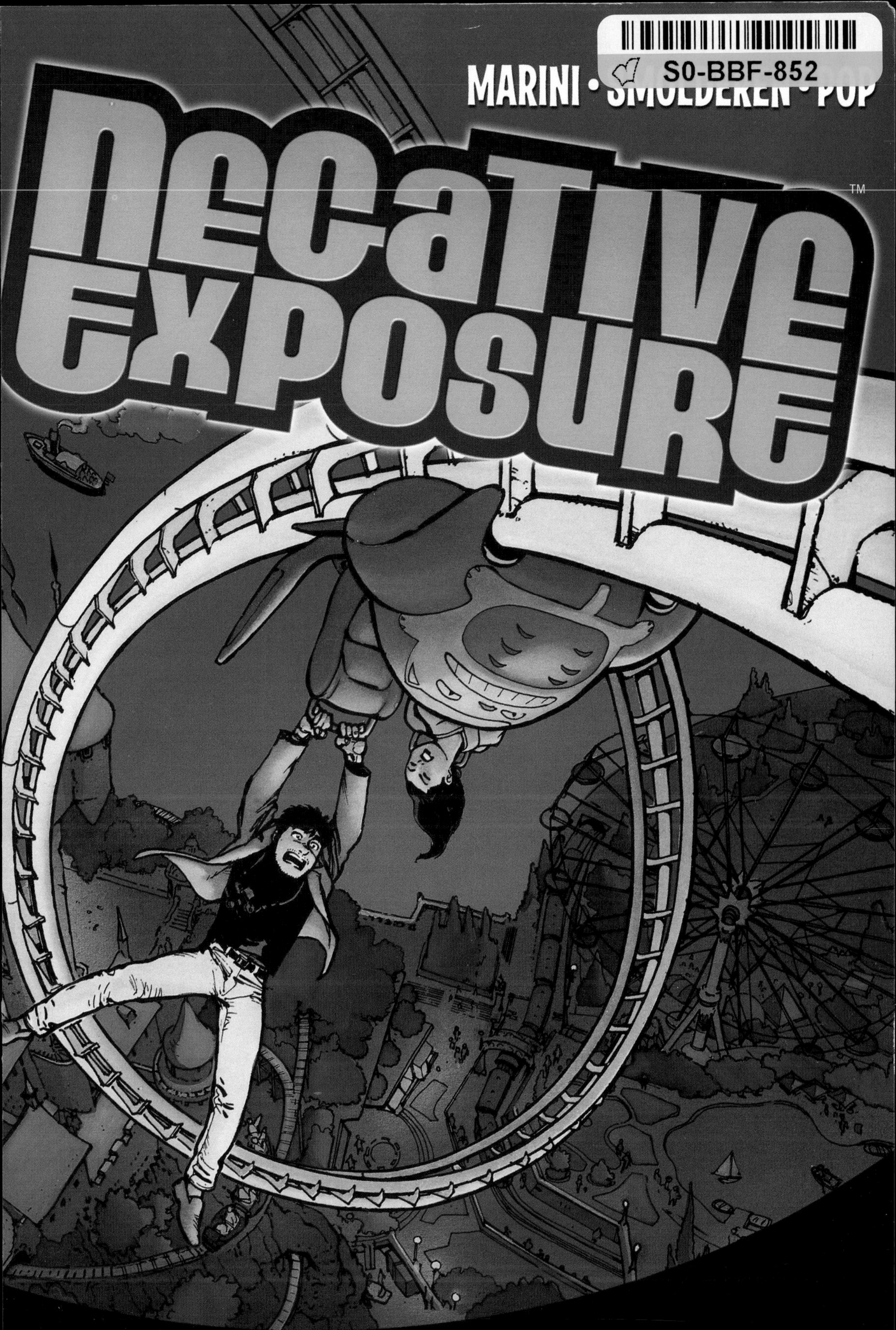

FEAR AND LOATHING IN KOKONINO WORLD

NEGATIVE EXPOSURE ™

Story: **THIERRY SMOLDEREN & POP**

Art: **ENRICO MARINI**

Colors: **GREG CRUZ & ENRICO MARINI**

Translation: **KIRK ANDERSON & LUCIANO STORTI**

Book Design: **THIERRY FRISSEN**

Lettering: **JASON WAHLER**

Managing Editor: **PAUL BENJAMIN**

Marketing Manager: **ROBERT SILVA**

Special Thanks: **STÉPHANE MARTINEZ & IAN SATTLER**

Publisher: **FABRICE GIGER**

Humanoids Publishing, PO Box 931658, Hollywood, CA 90094. Negative Exposure™, and the Negative Exposure logo, Humanoids Publishing™
and the Humanoids Publishing logo are trademarks of Les Humanoïdes Associés S.A., Geneva (Switzerland), registered in various categories and countries.

INTRODUCTION

Zany international adventures, hapless clumsy heroes, beautiful femme fatales, katana wielding ninjas, cool mecha robots...NEGATIVE EXPOSURE's got it all! In this European Manga-inspired graphic novel by MARINI, SMOLDEREN and POP, you'll be taken on a kooky "ALICE IN WONDERLAND" style experience crammed with all of the visual wonders and adrenaline inducing action sequences that have made Manga one of the world's most beloved forms of storytelling.

MARINI, SMOLDEREN and POP are clearly inspired by the best that Japanese comics have to offer. Their characters are reminiscent of the more realistic style many recent Manga titles have adopted since OTOMO's seminal AKIRA came out in the eighties. But unlike OTOMO's work, NEGATIVE EXPOSURE is as much a ridiculous comedy as it is an action adventure.

NEGATIVE EXPOSURE is Manga for an MTV generation. Like the ridiculous roller coasters in the fictional Kokonino World, the pacing in NEGATIVE EXPOSURE flips and twists in a refreshingly jolting way. MARINI, SMOLDEREN and POP deviously relish in keeping their readers constantly on their toes. Before the reader has a chance to become comfortable with a crime noir setup, the creators add element after element of comedic action that borrows from the great variety of Manga genres.

Before you turn the page and start reading, sit back, buckle up, and brace yourself for an insane, wild, and hysterical ride through a beautifully unpredictable example of Manga funneled through the crazed vision of three very talented European artists.

Enjoy.

UMPH!

FEAR AND LOATHING IN KOKONINO WORLD
Art by Enrico Marini, story by Thierry Smolderen

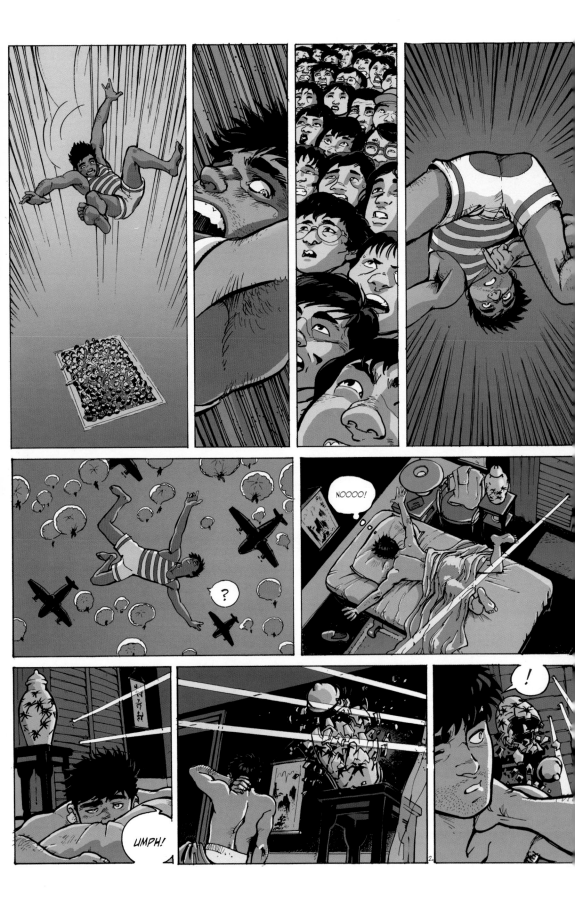

"SUNDAY, 9:00 P.M., ONE HUNDRED FIFTY METERS FROM TIANANMEN SQUARE...

...THE STUDENT UPRISING IS OVER...

...I HAVE NO WORDS TO DESCRIBE WHAT'S HAPPENING HERE..."

IS THAT FOR ME?

お夜食ここに置いときますよ

I DON'T UNDERSTAND...

...THANKS ANYWAY!

WHAT? THEY'RE EMPTY! WHAT DOES THAT MEAN?

THAT MEANS THAT YOU'D BETTER GET BACK TO WORK IF YOU WANT TO BE OF MORE USE THAN THOSE SHELLS!

YOU'RE A REPORTER, AREN'T YOU?

I'VE BEEN WONDERING THAT MYSELF.

WHO ARE YOU, MA'AM? WHERE DID YOU PARK YOUR FLYING SAUCER?

I'M FRIEND OF CHINA...

AND MY MERCEDES IS PARKED OVER THERE!

LIE DOWN BETWEEN THE SEATS!

AND DON'T MOVE AN INCH...

TO THE HOSPITAL, *QUICK! QUICK!*

NO *TIME* FOR THAT...

WE'VE GOT *BETTER* THINGS TO DO!

WITH FRIENDS LIKE YOU, CHINA DOESN'T NEED *ENEMIES!*

SHUT UP!

IF THE SOLDIERS FIND YOU, WE'LL BOTH HAVE A TERRIBLE SUMMER!

THERE ARE ROADBLOCKS *EVERY-WHERE,* BARRICADES IN FLAMES, TANKS, MILLIONS OF ENRAGED PEOPLE ...

I HOPE YOUR MERCEDES IS *WELL*-INSURED.

I'VE GOT THE BEST INSURANCE THERE IS...

IS THAT SO?

A PASS SIGNED BY OLD DENG HIMSELF!

BECAUSE YOU'RE ALSO A FRIEND OF DENG XIAOPING?

STOP ACTING LIKE A *MORON!* AFTER WHAT HAPPENED TODAY, DENG HAS NO MORE FRIENDS!

YOUR CAR IS FULL OF *WEIRD* STUFF!

WHAT'S WRITTEN ON THESE TOYS?

WELCOME TO *KOKONINO WORLD!*

KOKONINO WORLD?

THE FAMOUS JAPANESE AMUSEMENT PARK?

THAT'S THE ONE!

AHEM... MA'AM?

...BETWEEN TOURISTS, AND WITH THE UTMOST RESPECT...

...WHO ARE YOU, *REALLY,* AND *WHERE* ARE YOU TAKING ME?...

STOMP

STONG

SHIT

I *AM* MADAM KOKONINO!

...AND I'M GIVING YOU THE SCOOP OF YOUR *LIFE* ON A SILVER PLATTER...

UMPH...

I'M NOT SURE I REALLY *WANT* YOUR SCOOP, MADAME KOKONINO!

BEFORE MEETING YOU, I WAS SURROUNDED BY A REAL LIFE-SIZE REVOLUTION...

...BUT THAT'S A *TOTAL* "B MOVIE" ...

... I WOULDN'T MIND TAKING THINGS *EASY* FOR A WHILE!

THAT'S THE MAGIC OF KOKONINO WORLD STARTING TO TAKE EFFECT, MR. VARESE!

NOW GIVE ME A HAND WITH THE TARP!

...WHAT'S ON THE OTHER SIDE OF THE FENCE?

WHAT IS THIS SCOOP?

FIND A *GOOD* HIDING-PLACE!

THE TRUCKS WILL ARRIVE IN HALF AN HOUR!

AND THEN WHAT?

THEN YOU *JUMP* THE FENCE!

AND DON'T FORGET TO *LOAD* THE CAMERA!

TELL ME, MADAME KOKONINO?

STAY CALM, TRY TO TAKE THE BEST PICTURES YOU CAN...

AND ABOVE ALL, MR. VARESE...

UNDERSTAND THAT THERE'S *ABSOLUTELY NOTHING* YOU CAN DO FOR THOSE POOR DEVILS!

IF THE SOLDIERS FIND YOU, YOU'RE A *DEAD MAN!*

WHAT POOR DEVILS? WHAT ARE YOU *TALKING* ABOUT?

A MASS EXECUTION, MR. VARESE! TWO HUNDRED STUDENTS ARRESTED LAST NIGHT IN TIANANMEN SQUARE!

OH, NO!

I... I DON'T WANT TO SEE THAT, MA'AM!

I... I WON'T BE ABLE TO HANDLE IT!

TAKE THESE PHOTOS YOURSELF IF YOU HAVE TO!

I'M TOO SENSITIVE! I KNOW MOST OF THOSE STUDENTS!

MR. VARESE, STOP WHINING AND GET TO WORK!!

急げ

MADAME KOKONINO?

HUSH! THERE'S A TANK COMBING THE AREA!

ARE YOU NUTS? WHAT ARE YOU DOING?

MADAME KOKONINO!??

I'LL MAKE UP A STORY!

YOU HIDE AND MAKE SURE YOU GET THE PICTURES!

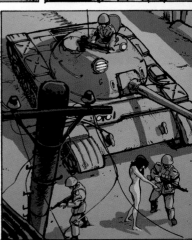

HELP! HELP!

HELP ME PLEASE!

VROO PORRR

HOOLIGANS! HOOLIGANS!

VROOR

THEY'RE GONE!

THANK YOUR FRIEND FOR ME...

...IT'S ME THEY'RE LOOKING FOR...

12

IT'S A KIND OF THRESHOLD!

I LEARNED THAT IN SCHOOL...

WHEN A SITUATION BECOMES INCOMPREHENSIBLE, YOU PASS THROUGH A "PSYCHOLOGICAL THRESHOLD"... THE CRITICAL MIND STOPS WORKING...

THEN THE BORDER BETWEEN REALITY AND HALLUCINATION FADES AWAY...

...YOU FALL INTO A DREAM WORLD...

...AND UNKNOWN FACES POP OUT FROM NOWHERE...

AH! I WAS WONDERING WHAT YOU WERE GETTING AT...

PEOPLE CALL ME "FRENCHMAN."

SORRY TO STARTLE YOU!

I'M VARESE!

...WHAT ARE YOU DOING AROUND HERE, MR. FRENCHMAN?

I HAD A LITTLE RUN-IN WITH AN ARMORED UNIT...

...WE WRECKED A FEW OF THEIR VEHICLES WITH SOME BUDDIES FROM THE UNIVERSITY...

AH, OK... THAT EXPLAINS EVERYTHING!

MADAME KOKONINO BROUGHT ME HERE.

SHE'S THE BABE WHO TOOK OFF WITH THE TANK!

SHE'S GOT ME TAKING PICTURES OF THE EXECUTIONS THAT ARE SUPPOSED TO HAPPEN HERE TONIGHT!

OH?! AND HOW DID SHE GET WIND OF THAT NEWS?

I HAVE NO IDEA. NO CLUE AT ALL...

...SHE CLAIMS TO BE A FRIEND OF DENG XIAOPING!

AH! WELL THERE YOU HAVE IT! JUST LIKE YOU SAY: THAT EXPLAINS EVERYTHING!

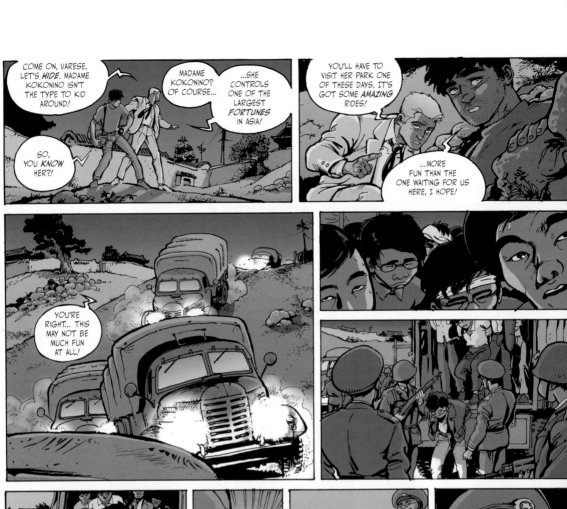

... MY GOD! ...I'M NOT FEELING SO GOOD... LET'S GET OUT OF HERE!

OK! LET'S GO! YOU'VE GOT YOUR PICTURES!

HOW DO YOU DO IT?

YOU DON'T EVEN LOOK *NERVOUS*, FRENCHMAN!

I'VE GOT A TRICK THAT *NEVER* FAILS IN THIS KIND OF SITUATION...

... WHEN THINGS GET *REALLY* UGLY...

I TELL MYSELF, IT'S ALL MADE UP, JUST AN *IDIOTIC* ATTRACTION...

...WE'RE STILL IN KOKONINO WORLD!

SO WHAT'S NEXT ON THE PROGRAM?

THE NEIGHBORHOOD IS NICE, BUT...

VROUOMVR

?

320

BROOOOOOAARRR

SHUT UP!

UMPH! HMM!

TPRRRRR

YEAR AFTER YEAR, THE SAME OLD MEN CLING TO POWER!

...THE DENGG, THE KHOMEINIS, THE CEAUSCESCUS.

NOTHING EVER CHANGES!

WHAT A SCREWED UP WORLD!

TLANK

I DON'T AGREE! FIRST, AS FAR AS I KNOW, NO ONE'S IMMORTAL!

AND 1989 ISN'T OVER YET...

THINGS COULD STILL MOVE IN THE RIGHT DIRECTION THIS FALL, IN EASTERN EUROPE!

YEAH, RIGHT! EASTERN EUROPE. EVEN WITH GORBY, NOTHING WILL CHANGE FOR A LEAST FIFTY YEARS!

I SEE...

... YOU REALLY DON'T BELIEVE IN CHANGE!

HEY! WHAT ARE YOU DOING?

FOLLO ME!

...BUT THE PICTURES IN THIS CAMERA...

...ARE GOING ON A WORLD TOUR AND WILL PUT OLD DENG OUT OF BUSINESS!

I'LL TAKE *FULL* RESPONSIBILITY FOR THAT!

SHIT! I NEVER SHOULD HAVE STOPPED AT THE HOTEL!

THE PLANE LEAVES IN FIFTEEN MINUTES!!

THANK YOU VERY MUCH.

GIVE MY BEST REGARDS TO MR. FRENCHMAN, OK?

HEY! *VARESE!*

!

SEEMS LIKE YOU GOT A *HELL* OF A SCOOP!

BEN, *BUDDY,* NEWS TRAVELS FAST!

I SAW BERNIE AT THE HOTEL, AFTER YOU PASSED BY...

...HE TOLD ME YOU LOOKED LIKE YOU'D JUST PHOTOGRAPHED A YETI!

SO, WHAT'D YOU GET FOR US?

AN EXCLUSIVE INTERVIEW WITH THE AYATOLLAH KHOMEINI!

THAT'S A GOOD ONE... HE DIED LAST NIGHT!

THERE YOU HAVE IT...

DAMN, DO I WANT TO BE BACK IN GENEVA!

AND TAKE A LOOK AT THESE PHOTOS!

HEY, WHAT...!?

HEY!

OH!

LET ME GO!

14

SIT DOWN, VARESE!

I READ YOUR ARTICLE LAST NIGHT...

JUST A *FEW* QUESTIONS, IF YOU DON'T MIND...

SHOOT, BOSS!

WELL, DO YOU KNOW *WHERE* IN BEIJING THE EXECUTIONS TOOK PLACE?

UM... I DON'T...

BUT I EXPLAIN HOW I WAS TAKEN THERE...

YOU *DON'T* KNOW!

AND THIS MADAME KOKONINO? HOW IS *SHE* CONNECTED TO THE LEADERSHIP IN CHINA?

UH...

...AND MORE SPECIFICALLY, WITH DENG XIAOPING!

I ...

... I DIDN'T HAVE THE *CHANCE* TO ASK HER.

...AND WHAT WAS *HE* DOING IN BEIJING DURING THE EVENTS?

THIRD QUESTION: WHO *IS* THIS MYSTERIOUS MR. FRENCHMAN?

WHO ARE THIS GENTLEMAN'S CHINESE FRIENDS?

WHAT'S THE *NAME* OF THEIR ORGANIZATION?

WHY DIDN'T YOU PUT *FILM* IN YOUR CAMERA?

UM...

YOU DON'T KNOW... ONE MORE QUESTION, MR. VARESE...

DO YOU REALLY WANT TO KEEP THIS JOB?!!

YOU'RE *REJECTING* MY ARTICLE?!

BUT, *DAMN*, IT'S ALL *TRUE*, I SWEAR!

YOU NEED A VACATION, VARESE... A *LONG*, RELAXING VACATION!

HERE, I'LL EVEN SUGGEST A FEW BOOKS TO READ...

"TWENTY YEARS AFTER" AND "ALL THE PRESIDENT'S MEN."

YOU MAY NOTICE A *SLIGHT* DIFFERENCE BETWEEN THESE TWO MASTERPIECES...

...IN MY OPINION, DUMAS WASN'T PRACTICING EXACTLY THE SAME CRAFT AS OUR COLLEAGUES FROM THE WASHINGTON POST.

WHICH LEADS US BACK TO THE FUNDAMENTAL QUESTION: WHAT DO YOU *THINK* YOU'RE DOING?

BOSS... I KNOW THIS *SEEMS* LIKE A SECOND-RATE NOVEL, BUT...

... I *DIDN'T* MAKE ANYTHING UP!

THEN YOU'RE AN IDIOT!

AND SINCE I BELIEVE IN NATURAL SELECTION, I CONSIDER IT MY DUTY TO *FIRE YOU!*

A JOURNALIST WHO *BLOWS* A SCOOP LIKE THIS HAS NO RIGHT TO BE *FESTERING* AROUND HERE...

...WHEN WE TAKE THE GARBAGE OUT EVERY DAY!

GOODBYE, VARESE!

SAY YOUR *PRAYERS*, COWBOY!

PLOP PLOP

OLIVIER VARÈSE
7, rue de Co...
1201 GENÈ...
SWITZERLAN...

VARÈSE

SO, VARESE, WHAT'S THE STORY?

OLIVER VARESE RETIRES IN JAPAN!

SMALL TOWN SWITZERLAND CAN *FINALLY* REST EASY!

IN JAPAN?

YEP!

MADAME KOKONINO, THE JAPANESE MULTIMILLIONAIRE, SENT ME A *FIRST CLASS* PLANE TICKET... AND I'VE GOT A HUNCH SHE'S GOT WORK FOR ME!

KOKONINO? LIKE THE JAPANESE CARTOONS?

YOU'VE HEARD OF THEM?

I'VE GOT A BUDDY WHO'S... A REAL FANATIC... HE COLLECTS *EVERYTHING* HE CAN FIND ON THE KOKONINO EMPIRE!

HEY! THAT'S *AWESOME!* COULD YOU INTRODUCE ME TO YOUR FRIEND?

COME ON! GET A MOVE ON!

ARE YOU RUNNING ON FUMES OR WHAT?

LITTLE IDIOT!

WAIT FOR ME!

VROM

SAMUEL?

HEY, SAM?

?

BANZAI!

HEY!

FLAP

UMPH!

POC POC POC

20

!

DON'T MAKE A MOVE, STRANGER!

24

YAAOOOEEE!

... THIS REPORTER HAS *SOMETHING* UP HIS SLEEVE, SINCE HE DIDN'T PUBLISH THEM...

NO... IF VARESE WANTS TO *NEGOTIATE* OVER THESE NEGATIVES, HE'LL HAVE TO FIND THE *COURAGE* TO SAY SO TO MY FACE...

HE'S ARRIVING ON THE SAME PLANE AS YOU ARE. KEEP AN EYE ON HIM...

...YES...

SSSSSSS...

SPLASSSHH

DOES YOUR SECRETARY *ALWAYS* TRAVEL SO MUCH?

THAT *DOESN'T* CONCERN YOU!

LET'S TALK ABOUT *THESE* LITTLE HORRORS...

HMM! AND IF SOMEONE GOT ONE OF THESE IN THE EYE? ...

NOT A PROBLEM. THEY'D *REALLY* HAVE TO BE INCREDIBLY STUPID TO...

CLIC

BOING

AY!

KYI! TAKE MR. NAKATSU! WE'RE CHANGING MERCHANDISING DIRECTORS!

BUT... BUT... THIS WAS YOUR HUSBAND'S IDEA!

CERTAINLY NOT! ... MY HUSBAND *HATED* DANGEROUS TOYS!

AH? THEN HE MADE A BIG MISTAKE MARRYING YOU!

KYI! TO THE ROCKET!

WHAT?

NO! YOU CAN'T!

NOOO!

I'VE BEEN WANTING TO USE THAT MISSILE TO GET RID OF AN INEPT EMPLOYEE FOR YEARS!

YOU'RE CRAZY!

Hi Hi Hi

Hi Hi Hi

NOOOO!

SSSSSS

SSSHH

GOODBYE, MR. NAKATSU!

AAAAH!

AAAAH!

OOOH! WOW!

AAAH!

AH! AH! AH!

DUMP HIM ANYWHERE... ON A MOUNTAINTOP, FOR EXAMPLE...

BRAVO! COOL!

I HATE IT WHEN PEOPLE MOCK ME!

KEEP SLEEPING! ... IN THREE HOURS, YOU'LL BE ...

... IN TOKYO!

YOUR SUITE IS RESERVED FOR THREE NIGHTS, MR. VARESE!

MADAME KOKONINO WILL SEND A CAR IN THE MORNING FOR YOUR MEETING.

OKAY, THANKS.

OH! A SUITE!

HAVE YOU ORDERED GEISHAS, AS LONG AS YOU'RE HERE?

YES, HALF A DOZEN.

MARVELOUS! ONE NIGHT WITH THEM AND YOU'LL BE A MASTER OF ORIGAMI! HA! HA! HA!

WOW! THIS LADY KOKONINO DOESN'T DO THINGS HALFWAY...

IS THIS A BATHTUB? OR A PIRANHA FARM?

TOC! TOC! TOC!

UM... COME IN?

?

I... THINK THIS MUST BE A MISTAKE...

NO! NO! NO MISTAKE...

...PRETTY PRESENT FOR HONORED GUEST!

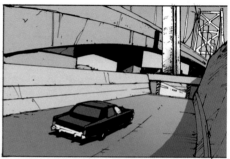

Biizzzzz

WELL, *HERE* WE ARE!

THANK YOU!

MR. VARÈSE? MADAME KOKONINO IS EXPECTING YOU...

THAT'S VERY KIND OF HER...

FOLLOW ME!

MADAME KOKONINO, YOUR ROBOT IS *INCREDIBLE!*

WHAT A *PLEASURE* TO SEE YOU AGAIN!

GULP!

AFTER YOU.

WHERE ARE THE PHOTOS, VARÈSE?

THE PHOTOS? WHAT PHOTOS?

DON'T MOCK ME.

IT'S *NOT* A GOOD DAY.

KYI!

BIB

VROODO

BUT...

WHAT? WHERE? I ...

SSSHHHOOOMM

ROLLER COASTERS!

MADAME KOKONINO, *STOP* THIS RIGHT AWAY!

はあ！

PLEASE STOP IT!

I HATE ...

KRIK KRIK

RRATATATATA

... ROLLER COASTERS!

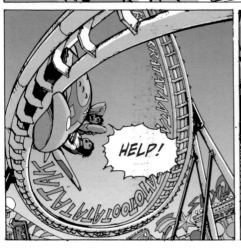

RRATATATATAAK

HELP!

AAAAHHH

ROTOTATATATAK

VRROOTOTO

HELP! HOW DO YOU *BUCKLE* INTO THESE... THESE...

SORRY!

GUESTS AREN'T *ENTITLED* TO SEATBELTS...

YOU'RE *CRAZY!* I'LL BE *THROWN OUT...*

NO, MR. VARÈSE. THE CENTRIFUGAL FORCE WILL KEEP YOU IN YOUR SEAT...

...AS LONG AS WE *KEEP* MOVING...

PRATATATATATAKK

CLANG!

?!

AAAAAHHH

OH! OH! OH! OH!

SO, MR. VARÈSE, THE *PHOTOS...?*

OH SHIT! SHIT! SHIT!

MADAME KOKONINO... I *NEVER* PUT *FILM* IN THE CAMERA...

I DON'T BELIEVE YOU, MR. VARÈSE!

THERE *NEVER* WERE ANY *PHOTOS!!!*

NO ONE COULD BE SO ABSENT-MINDED!

I COULD! I SWEAR TO YOU, I'VE DONE WORSE!

IN THAT CASE, YOU GET OFF HERE!

SCRATCH, SCRATCH

NNOOOOOOOONN

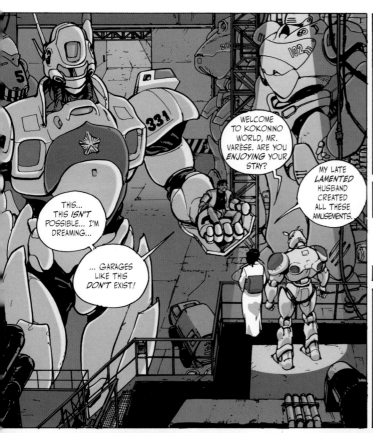

WELCOME TO KOKONINO WORLD, MR. VARÈSE. ARE YOU *ENJOYING* YOUR STAY?

THIS... THIS *ISN'T* POSSIBLE... I'M DREAMING...

... GARAGES LIKE THIS *DON'T* EXIST!

MY LATE *LAMENTED* HUSBAND CREATED ALL THESE AMUSEMENTS.

UNFORTUNATELY, I DON'T HAVE TIME TO SHOW YOU THE WHOLE SET...

I'M SURE YOU WOULD HAVE *ENJOYED* THE MORAY EEL POOL!

THAT DEPENDS ON WHETHER YOU'D BE IN YOUR BATHING SUIT, MADAME KOKONINO!

HEE...HEE... HEE...

ENOUGH, KY!!

I NEEDED TO SEE THOSE PHOTOS *PUBLISHED*, MR. VARÈSE!

OLD MAN DENG *COULDN'T* HAVE WITHSTOOD THE SCANDAL...

...I WOULD HAVE SHOWERED YOU WITH GOLD IF YOU PROVIDED ME THAT SERVICE...

!

I DON'T KNOW WHAT'S KEEPING ME FROM HAVING THAT ROBOT *CRUSH* YOU BETWEEN ITS FINGERS...

YOU... YOU...

UNTIL TOMORROW MORNING, MR. VARÈSE. I'LL GIVE YOUR *PUNISHMENT* SOME THOUGHT!

WHAT A *SADIST!*

AND A *MEGALOMANIAC* TO BOOT!

39

41

WATCH YOUR STEP!

THERE'S NO SAFETY NET FOR THIS ACT...

THANKS FOR REMINDING ME!

FRENCHMAN, I'M *SLIPPING*...

HERE IT IS, TAKE A LOOK!

HERE, YOU'LL HEAR BETTER WITH THIS!

PUFF!

PUFF!

PUFF!

I'VE BEEN A FAITHFUL SPECTATOR OF THEIR MEETINGS FOR FOUR YEARS...

I HAVEN'T MISSED ONE SINCE THEY THOUGHT THEY KILLED ME!

I KNOW... IT'S FRUSTRATING, BUT THERE'S NOTHING WE CAN DO.

WE'LL HAVE TO COMPROMISE WITH HIM!

DAMN IT!

WHOUM

CALM DOWN... HE'LL BE HERE IN A FEW MINUTES!

WHAT ARE WE GOING TO OFFER HIM IN EXCHANGE FOR FENG DING?

THE RESUMPTION OF INVESTMENTS...

... BUT WE'LL HAVE TO WORK ON CONGRESS FOR THAT...

I THINK I CAN CONVINCE MAGGY TO HOLD BACK ON THE HONG KONG ISSUE!

DAMN IT! IF ONLY YOU'D RECOVERED THE PHOTOS, MISS KOKONINO!

DO YOU REALIZE WHAT WE'RE GOING TO HAVE TO GIVE HIM?

SHH... HE'S HERE...

WHO ARE THEY TALKING ABOUT?

LOOK!

43

PERFECT! WE'RE SAFE!

THIS ONBOARD COMPUTER WILL OPEN ALL THE DOORS FOR US.

THEY LEFT THROUGH EXIT Z 109, MADAME KOKONINO!

Z 109?!

HOW DO THEY KNOW ABOUT THAT SHORTCUT?

WHO'S DRIVING THE CAR? WHO IS NEXT TO VARÈSE?

FRENCHMAN, FOR PITY'S SAKE, WATCH WHERE YOU'RE GOING!

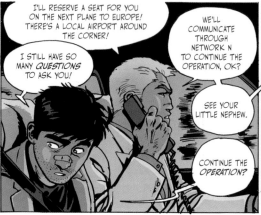

I'LL RESERVE A SEAT FOR YOU ON THE NEXT PLANE TO EUROPE! THERE'S A LOCAL AIRPORT AROUND THE CORNER!

I STILL HAVE SO MANY QUESTIONS TO ASK YOU!

WE'LL COMMUNICATE THROUGH NETWORK N TO CONTINUE THE OPERATION, OK?

SEE YOUR LITTLE NEPHEW.

CONTINUE THE OPERATION?

WE'LL HAVE TO FREE OUR FRIEND, FENG DING, THE BIOLOGIST...

SINCE DENG XIAOPING WILL TURN HIM OVER TO MADAME KOKONINO!

WE'LL MEET AGAIN, MR. VARÈSE! THAT'S A PROMISE!

46

HEY!

?

WHERE ARE YOU TAKING ME?!

HEY!

OW!

HELP!

WHAT ARE YOU DOING?

I'M IN TRANSIT!

CRACK!

THAT CERTAINLY DOESN'T ENTITLE YOU TO SEARCH...

...MY THINGS!

NO! THIS IS A SET UP!

LET ME GO!

HEY!

SOMEONE IS OUT TO GET ME!

!

MMPF

IT'S HIM!

HE MUST'VE PLANTED IT ON THE PLANE!

GET HIM!

NOW I UNDERSTAND EVERYTHING!

HE WORKS FOR MADAME KOKONINO!

TOC

OWW!

GOOD GOD!

JUST TEN GRAMS OF H? ANOTHER *SMALL-TIMER!*

CLA-CLAC

ALRIGHT, I'LL TAKE IT!

MR. ... UH... VARÈSE, IS THAT IT?

?!

VÉRONIQUE!

YOUR CONSULATE JUST CALLED ME. I AM A LAWYER AND...

VÉRONIQUE?! YOU... YOU DON'T *REMEMBER* ME?

IN THE PLANE, A FEW DAYS AGO?

HMM? NO.

I'M *TERRIBLE* WITH FACES...

AH? YOU HAVEN'T LOOKED OUT THE WINDOW YET?

LISTEN, MR. VARÈSE, I'M NOT IN THE HABIT OF GETTING PERSONAL WITH MY CLIENTS.

IN TWO HOURS I HAVE TO ATTEND AN EXECUTION AND...

BUT, THAT'S *NOT* POSSIBLE...

AN EXECUTION?

45

MAMMA MIA!

WHOA! COME LOOK AT THIS, PHIL!

OH! SHIT! FUCK A DUCK!

POOR GUY! HE WENT FLYING, CAN YOU IMAGINE?!

...THE PALACE IS *300 METERS* FROM HERE!

BAH! BEATS BEING *HANGED!*

I HOPE I'M AS BRAVE AS *YOU* WHEN MY DAY COMES!

I'M USED TO THE IDEA, THAT'S ALL!

BY THE WAY, WHAT ABOUT YOUR LETTER? ANY *NEWS* FROM THE REAL WORLD?

PING! TZOING! TIGILING TZOING, TZOING!

HAAAAPPY BIRTHDAY TO YOOOUUU!

WHO COULD HAVE SENT ME THIS PIECE OF *CRAP?*

THE LETTER ISN'T EVEN SIGNED...

SEVEN MONTHS LATE... WELL, IT'S THE *THOUGHT* THAT...

HELLO, VARÈSE! FRENCHMAN HERE!

LISTEN CAREFULLY: CONTACT RED LAMASSEAU AS SOON AS POSSIBLE! HE'S BEING HELD IN YOUR PRISON...

...TELL HIM YOU ARE LEAVING TOGETHER. "TUNA FISH" WILL BE WAITING FOR BOTH OF YOU AT THE MEETING POINT!

TELL ME, FRENCHMAN, HOW ARE OUR PLANS GOING?

IF ALL GOES WELL, WE'LL HAVE OUR SWISS JOURNALIST BACK WITHIN TWO DAYS...

PERFECT. AND THE CHINESE BIOCHEMIST?

I'M ON HIS TAIL EVERY TIME HE GOES OUT, HOPING TO GET A WORD WITH HIM...

WE HAVE TO BE CAREFUL.

AND PATIENT...

EXCELLENT. YOU KNOW WHERE TO FIND ME WITH ANY NEWS.

COME IN!

I DIDN'T EXPECT TO SEE YOU TODAY... THE REBELS HAVE BLOWN UP THE PALACE...

YES, I HEARD THE NEWS!

ANYWAY... THE PRESIDENT IS SAFE. LIFE GOES ON.

IF YOU CAN CALL IT THAT...

AREN'T YOU WELL, VARÈSE? YOU'RE LOOKING A LITTLE SQUALID TODAY...

THEY'RE EXECUTING MY CELLMATE AT DAWN!

OH?

HMM! ... THE NEWS ISN'T GOOD FOR YOU EITHER, MY FRIEND!

I TICKLE YOUR NOSTRILS, MADAME KOKONINO!

I MUST *REALLY* ANNOY YOU!

IF YOUR EELS EAT MY FEET, I'LL NEED A SMALLER SIZE SHOE!

GO *SUCK* A PENGUIN EGG!

OLIVER!

WHAT!

YOU'RE *NOT* GONNA BELIEVE THIS!

THEY REPLACED MY EXECUTION WITH A BASKETBALL GAME!

IT LOOKS LIKE THEY'VE PICKED THOSE OF US WHO ARE STILL IN DECENT SHAPE TO PLAY AGAINST THE REBELS.

BUT *WHY?*

SINCE WHEN ARE THEY ORGANIZING TOURNAMENTS IN THIS PIGSTY?

NO IDEA! UH OH! THEY'RE BRINGING OUT "THE MOUNTAIN"!

THE MOUNTAIN?

YEAH... RED LAMASSEAU, THE HIPPY KILLER!

GIMME THAT, YOU PUNK!

HERE WE GO! THERE'S THE REASON FOR THIS HAPPY CHANGE OF PLANS...

OBSERVERS FROM THE RED CROSS! *DAMN RIGHT* A BASKETBALL GAME WILL LEAVE THEM WITH A BETTER TASTE IN THEIR MOUTHS THAN A HANGING...

AND IT WILL FOR ME TOO!

LOOK! THAT'S DIM SUM, THE INSURGENT LEADER!

YOU THINK THE REBELS WEED OUT THEIR RECRUITS?

ANYBODY OVER FIVE FEET GOES STRAIGHT TO THE JUNGLE!

DAMMIT! *SHUT UP OR I'LL RIP YOUR HEAD OFF!*

TWIIIT FLAP

GRR!

HERE, RED!

PASS! PASS!

. HEY! YO! YOU GOT STICKY FINGERS?

SO, HE'S PLAYING SOLO?

TUMB TUMB TUMB

PLOP PLOP

SPAK WROARR

UMPF!

HEY!

LOOK AT THAT! THE BIG GUY'S RUNNING AWAY!

LET'S GO! FOLLOW HIM!

IT BEATS STICKING AROUND FOR THE HALF-TIME SHOW!

HEY!

WAIT! YO! RED!!

STAY BACK, VARÈSE! LET GO!

VÉRONIQUE?!

59

SHIT! I WARNED YOU!

VROOAAR

OLIVER, HOP ON!

VRN VRN

FOLLOW THEM! DON'T LOSE THEM!

VRR VRRN

YOU THINK THEY HAVE A PLAN?

ROOAAAIRR

YOU'LL NEVER GUESS WHO'S DRIVING THE TRUCK!

YEAH! IT'S THE ESCAPE I WAS SUPPOSED TO BE PART OF!

WHO?!

MY LAWYER! YOU COULD SAY SHE'S THE PERFECT MATCH FOR THE BEAST!

TATA TA TAK TAK

?!

VRRRN

VÉRONIQUE! VÉRONIQUE! WHO WOULD HAVE THOUGHT?!

AY!

GET DOWN!

!

HALT!

OWW!

SKRIIII

AAAAH!

YAHOOOO

VRRRr

60

RATATTAK BRATTAK

NOOOO!

YES!

VROOAMM

RRROARRR

NOT TOO SHABBY...

SO, COULD YOU DO THAT AGAIN FOR PHOTOGRAPHERS?

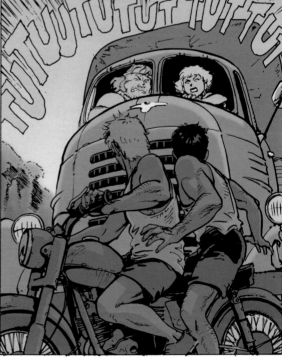

TUTUTUTUT TUTTUT

BEATS BEING HANGED AT DAWN, RIGHT?

WAAAH!

TUTUTUTUT

61

CHAK CHAK

CHAK

SHIT! HE'S *CUTTING* THE BRIDGE LOOSE!

HOLY SHIT!

WHAT ARE YOU THINKING!

GRRR!

CHAK

ARE YOU CRAZY?!

BLAM

SLAK

VÉRONIQUE! DAMN...

ARRGH!

ARRGH!

Riiii

DON'T COME ANY CLOSER! OR THIS BRIDGE IS GOING *DOWN!*

MY BUDDY JUST TOOK THE BIG JUMP BECAUSE OF *YOU!*

YOU'VE BEEN ON OUR ASS SINCE WE LEFT THE PRISON!

NOBODY ASKED YOU ALONG, BUDDY!

WRONG! I HAVE AN EXCELLENT REASON TO FOLLOW YOU...

I'VE GOT A MEETING WITH TUNA FISH! IMAGINE THAT! IF YOU'D LET ME EXPLAIN...

WITH TUNA FISH?

THAT CHANGES *EVERYTHING!* WELCOME TO THE TEAM!

SORRY ABOUT YOUR FRIEND, BUDDY...

IF ONLY LIFE WERE SIMPLE, HUH, WITHOUT THESE LITTLE MISUNDERSTANDINGS.

POOR PHIL... OH WELL...

AT LEAST HE ESCAPED THE ROPE... FOR WHAT THAT'S WORTH...

63

GET UP, BUDDY! YOU'RE JUST ON TIME! WE'RE SAVED!

POOR GUY, HOW DID YOU *SURVIVE* THAT FALL?

SAVED!

HELLO! IS EVERYTHING OK?

C-CROD

C'MON, PHIL... WE'RE ALMOST THERE!

O... OLIVER ... TELL THEM TO *WATCH OUT!* THERE'S AN ARMY CUTTER UPSTREAM!

WHAT?

BAWHDOOM

C-CRE

SHIT!

VRRR TAK TAKATAK

HANG ON KIDS!

SHIT! MOVE IT!

POW POW POW

ALL ABOARD? WE'RE OUTTA HERE!!

TOKA TOKA

YAHOO!

TOKA TOKA

ATATATAK

VRRRRRR

POW POW POW

BY THE WAY, WHERE'S THIS PLANE TAKING US? ...

TO PANAWAN ISLAND, IN THE PHILIPPINES!

LATER

DAMN, MADAME KOKONINO, YOU FINALLY GOT ME WHERE YOU WANT ME.

BUT I TOLD YOU THERE WASN'T *ANY* FILM IN THE CAMERA!

HERE'S WHAT'S LEFT OF MY LAST VICTIM, VARÈSE!

OH HA, HA... VERY FUNNY...

PANAWAN ISLAND

IS VARÈSE IN THERE? I'M THE FRENCHMAN.

AH, SO *YOU'RE* THE GUY WHO SENT THE BIRTHDAY CARD SEVEN MONTHS LATE?

WHAT ARE YOU GOING TO DO WITH HIM?

I'M TAKING HIM TO JAPAN ON SOME BUSINESS.

WIDOW KOKONINO?

HE *TOLD* YOU ABOUT HER?

EVEN IN HIS SLEEP, SHE'S ALL HE TALKS ABOUT... *GO EASY* ON OLIVER! WE ALL TOOK A FEW HITS IN KANTOUCHA!

BZZ! VACATION! BZZ!

DON'T WORRY! WE'LL TAKE *GOOD* CARE OF HIM!

ZZZ...

HUH? WHAT'S GOING...

FRENCHMAN?

COME TAKE A LOOK, VARÈSE!

WHAT DO YOU THINK? NICE VIEW, HUH?

HOW IS THIS *POSSIBLE*? WE WERE IN A SEAPLANE, AND THEN...

YOU'VE BEEN SLEEPING FOR *24 HOURS!* WHAT WOULD YOU SAY TO A FEAST IN THE *BEST* RESTAURANT IN TOWN?

KOKONINO WORLD!

WELL, *SURE!* I FEEL LIKE I COULD EAT A SUMO WRESTLER!

WHERE SHOULD I START? I'VE GOT A HUNDRED QUESTIONS FOR YOU!

CALM DOWN, VARÈSE! EVERYTHING WILL BE CLEAR IN DUE TIME!

WOW! WHAT'S THAT ELECTRONIC GADGET DO?

I TOOK THIS OFF OF MADAME KOKONINO'S MERCEDES! WITH THIS WE CAN KEEP AN EYE ON ALL THE PARK'S EXITS!

WHAT HAPPENED HERE WHILE I WAS GONE, FRENCHMAN? WHAT ABOUT THAT BIOCHEMIST THEY WERE GETTING OUT OF CHINA?

FENG DING? HE'S BEEN WORKING FOR THE WIDOW SINCE NOVEMBER!

SKRiii!

IF WE DON'T MOVE FAST, MADAME KOKONINO COULD BE DEALING OUT ETERNITY TO WORLD LEADERS...

DOES THAT MAKE YOU SMILE, VARÈSE?

SO, WHAT'S YOUR PLAN?

NO, I'D SAY THAT WAS MORE OF A *GRIMACE!*

I HOPE YOU'RE NOT THINKING OF KIDNAPPING THE SCIENTIST?

THEY ORGANIZE EXCURSIONS FOR HIM OUTSIDE THE COMPOUND, WITH GOOD SECURITY... I'M WAITING FOR THE CHANCE TO TALK TO HIM.

NICE ATMOSPHERE...

YOU THINK SO? THERE'S A TABLE OVER THERE.

I DON'T LIKE THE LOOK OF SOME OF THE CUSTOMERS.

FENG DING IS UNAWARE OF THE SECRET AGREEMENT BETWEEN MADAME KOKONINO AND DENG XIAOPING.

WE'LL SEE HOW HE REACTS WHEN HE FINDS OUT WHO HE'S *REALLY* WORKING FOR!

AAAAH! OOOOH!

OK! HMM... EVEN THE PRICES IN YEN SEEM APPETIZING...

AAAAHH!

!

CRACK

AAHRG

KA-POW

KA-POW

KA-POW

WHAT THE *HELL* IS GOING ON?

PROBABLY A SETTLING OF SCORES BETWEEN TWO RIVAL GANGS.

KA-POW

THE BODY THEY DUMPED ON THE TERRACE IS PROBABLY A TRAITOR...

BLAM BLAM BLAM

WHAT DO YOU SAY WE FIND ANOTHER RESTAURANT?

YOU! GO PLAY SOMEWHERE ELSE!

WOW! JUST OUR LUCK!

CHAK

GOOD *IDEA!*

MMM... THESE TELE-*NINJAS AREN'T* AS PHONY AS I THOUGHT...

BANG AAH BLAM

IAAAH

THESE *TELE-NINJAS!?*

YEAH, THAT'S WHAT THEY CALL THEM...

BLAM BLAM

YOUNG CRIMINALS INSPIRED MORE BY *TV SERIES* THAN THE MARTIAL ARTS *TRADITION!*

SETTLING SCORES AROUND THE CORNER FROM KOKONINO WORLD! I WONDER IF THERE'S A CONNECTION!

OK! I SEE THE FUN'S NOT OVER YET!

4:00 A.M.... FRENCHMAN'S SNORING.
THAT REASSURES ME A LITTLE...

THE DAY THAT WITCH GETS HER IMMORTALITY
SERUM, THERE'LL BE NO STOPPING HER!

STRANGE, I NEVER MANAGE TO ASK HIM
THE RIGHT QUESTIONS AT THE RIGHT TIME.
I KNOW ALMOST NOTHING ABOUT HIM... ANYWAY...
WHAT DOES IT MATTER?! HE GOT ME OUT OF
KANTOUCHA, AND HE'S CONSPIRING AGAINST
WIDOW KOKONINO... KNOCK ON WOOD...

ALREADY
AT WORK?

I DIDN'T
SLEEP
LAST
NIGHT!

TSK, TSK! YOU'VE GOT
TO TAKE CARE OF YOURSELF, FENG!
DON'T HESITATE TO GET SOME FRESH
AIR FROM TIME TO TIME...

I'D LIKE TO MEDITATE IN
NATURE... THERE'S A LITTLE
TEMPLE ON THE MOUNTAIN.
COULD YOU TAKE ME THERE?

21

THE... THE LITTLE TEMPLE?
BUT OF COURSE... NAPPIER WILL TAKE YOU
THERE WHENEVER YOU LIKE...

RIGHT NOW
THEN?

AT YOUR
SERVICE!
WILL YOU BE
JOINING US,
MADAME
KOKONINO?

NOT TODAY...

YOU'LL LIKE
THAT PLACE,
FENG.

AN INVITING PLACE FOR LOVERS...
AND VISIONARIES...

71

SO, IT SEEMS I SNORE...

WHAT?

OH! YOU FOUND MY NOTES?

AND ALL THE QUESTIONS YOU HAVE ABOUT ME!

WELL, SINCE YOU BRING IT UP...

NOW YOU KNOW HOW MUCH I LIKE YOU...

UH OH! THERE'S MOVEMENT. THEY'RE LEAVING!

PUT ON YOUR WIG... WE'RE TAILING THEM!

WHAT ARE THEY DOING? COMING UP HERE?

OF COURSE! THE LITTLE TEMPLE!

THIS IS CRAZY. I FEEL LIKE AN *IDIOT* AS A BLOND. I SHOULD'VE TAKEN THE PRIEST DISGUISE!

OW!

THIS TIME, WE'VE *GOT* HIM!

I'VE GOT THE FEELING SHE CAME HERE WITH HER HUSBAND BEFORE HE BUILT THE AMUSEMENT PARK!

WHAT ARE YOU TALKING ABOUT?

MADAME KOKONINO, OF COURSE... SHE SPOKE OF A PLACE FOR VISIONARIES AND LOVERS...

WILL YOU WAIT FOR ME HERE, MR. NAPPIER?

AS YOU WISH...

NO OFFENSE, BUT THAT WIG SUITS YOU LIKE A BOOT IN THE ASS... TRY TO STAY LOW PROFILE!

I GET IT. STAY PUT.

HOW OLD DO YOU THINK SHE IS?

?

... MAYBE SIXTY YEARS OLD... STILL A LITTLE GIRL!

SHE'LL BURY US ALL! ... UNLESS WE BENEFIT FROM YOUR WORK...

AH HA! *NICE* INTRODUCTION!

WHAT DO YOU KNOW ABOUT MY WORK?

?

I UNDERSTAND THAT ONE OF THE FIRST TO BENEFIT FROM IT WILL BE DENG XIAOPING!

IF THE DEVIL LETS HIM LIVE THAT LONG!

SORRY, FENG DING, BUT THAT'S THE *TRUTH!* THE BUTCHER OF TIANANMEN SQUARE DIDN'T GIVE YOU TO YOUR NEW BOSS WITHOUT CONDITIONS!

MADAME KOKONINO WAS RIGHT... THIS PLACE *IS* MAGICAL.

CURIOUS, ISN'T IT, HOW SOME THINGS FIND THEIR PLACE IN ETERNITY QUITE NATURALLY!

THAT'S TRUE.

THE FURTHER I GET IN MY RESEARCH, THE MORE RESPECT I HAVE FOR THOSE THINGS...

TOUMB!

HUH?

HA! HA! HA!

BOO!

AAAH!

HA! HA! HA!

WHAT THE...

HEY! THAT'S A MONK!?

WOUP
WOUP

OH!

WOUP
WOUP

WHAT'S THIS CLOWNING AROUND?

DO YOU GET YOUR JOLLIES PUTTING DENTS IN CARS?

WOUP!

HEY! I'M TALKING TO YOU, YOU BUNCH OF CLOWNS!

OK! WE'LL SEE WHAT THE FRENCHMAN HAS TO SAY ABOUT THIS!

HA! HA! HA!

DRIIING
DRIIING

HELLO? SHIRO HERE!

STUPID PIECE OF SHIT!

I GAVE YOU AN ORDER NOT TO MOVE ON THE YAKUZA BEFORE OUR DEAL...

BUT "WHITE SWORD"...

...WAS *CLOSED!* I TURN ON THE TV AND I FIND OUT YOU ATTACKED THEM YESTERDAY!

AND RIGHT AROUND THE CORNER FROM KOKONINO WORLD! YOU WILL BE *PUNISHED,* SHIRO!

YES... "WHITE SWORD."

CLIC!

DONE WITH YOUR MEDITATION?

DID YOU ENJOY THIS PLACE?

VERY MUCH, THANK YOU.

SO, DID YOU SEE THE MONASTERY SCHOOL IN ACTION?

I KNOW... THE MASTER SOMETIMES GETS A LITTLE CLOSE TO THE FOURTH DIMENSION...

I COULDN'T BELIEVE MY *EYES!*

THEY WERE JUMPING AND MOVING AROUND *IN A FLASH...*

FENG DING HAS ASKED ME FOR 24 HOURS TO THINK... IF HE'S GOING TO LEAVE, HE'LL ARRANGE TO VISIT THE OTAKE MUSEUM THE DAY AFTER TOMORROW...

THE OTAKE MUSEUM? ...

THERE'S A DISCREET EXIT... OUR FRIEND WILL ONLY HAVE TO GO THROUGH ONE DOOR TO GET AWAY FROM MADAME KOKONINO!

COULD YOU TAKE ME TO THE MAIN ENTRANCE? I'D LIKE TO VISIT THE PARK...

VISIT THE PARK? *OF COURSE!* I'VE GOT A PASS IF YOU'D LIKE TO TAKE A SUBMARINE TOUR...

BY THE WAY... HOW IS YOUR RESEARCH GOING? DO YOU THINK IT WILL BE LONG?

NAPPIER, YOU ASK ME THAT QUESTION *AT LEAST* TWICE A DAY!

OH, *SORRY!*

NO, I SWEAR TO YOU, MAN! IT'S *MUCH* BETTER ON YOU THAN THE BLOND WIG!

I DON'T KNOW. I DON'T KNOW!

AS A GENERAL RULE, I *DON'T* DO VERY WELL WITH DISGUISES!

PEOPLE SAY I'M A LITTLE *AWKWARD* ALL BY MYSELF, SO WHEN I TRY TO DRESS UP...

DON'T GET A *COMPLEX.* YOU'LL PASS THE TEST!

OH! A *HANDSOME* YOUNG PRIEST!

HEY! HEY!

OH! OH!

HA! HA! AND BRILLIANTLY AT THAT!

DAMN! HE'S LATE!

FRENCHMAN!

IT'S HIM! IT'S HIM!

THE MAN WHO HID THE JUNK IN MY CAMERA! GOOD GOD, I'D LIKE TO GET MY *HANDS* ON HIM!

HIM? BUT THAT'S NAPPIER, WIDOW KOKONINO'S SECRETARY! HE'S A NOTORIOUS HALFWIT!

HE WOULDN'T HURT A FLY!

LISTEN, I'LL BET YOU A *HAVANA CIGAR* THAT I'VE GOT HIM TO THANK FOR MY ONE-YEAR SABBATICAL IN PRISON!

WHATEVER. WE'VE GOT TO MOVE, AND FAST! YOU TAKE THIS HALL, THEN GO DOWN THE STAIRS BEHIND THE SHOWCASE AND WAIT FOR US THERE!

THERE'S JUST ONE DOOR TO GET THROUGH... NOW *GO*, VARÈSE.

HOW ARE YOU GOING TO MAKE FENG DING DISAPPEAR?

CLAP CLAP CLAP

HUH? THE STAIRS, BEHIND WHICH SHOWCASE?

?!

BOUM!

HEY!

SHIT! SHIT! SHIT!

CLAP CLAP CLAP

NAPPIER!

VARÈSE?!

WOK!

JUGK

SURPRISE! THE SUCKER IS ALIVE!

AHG!

I WON'T BE LONG...

MY GOD!

OOPS!

OKAY: WE'RE DONE! THANKS AND GOODBYE!

CLAP CLAP CLAP

KA-POW

KA-POW

79

80

ALLOW ME, FATHER. ... CAN I HELP YOU?

IN THE CAR, QUICK! ... I DON'T WANT TO HEAR A PEEP OUT OF YOU 'TIL WE GET TO KOKONINO WORLD! ...

GOT IT?

IF YOU SO MUCH AS *OPEN* YOU MOUTH, EVEN TO SING *EDELWEISS,* I'LL TURN YOU INTO AN OCARINA!

LET'S GO, NAPPIER!

SEE YOU SOON, MR. VARÈSE...

NOW YOU CAN TALK! ... WHAT WERE YOU DOING IN THE *MUSEUM?*

WHO ARE YOU WORKING WITH?

HOW DID YOU GET OUT OF THE HOLE IN KANTOUCHA?

EDELWEISS...

EDELW...

31

WELL, MR. VARÈSE, WE MEET *AGAIN!*

DO YOU LIKE *ROBOTS?*

!

CAN YOU IMAGINE? THESE HAVE NEVER BEEN SHOWN TO THE PUBLIC...

MY HUSBAND DESIGNED THIS ATTRACTION JUST BEFORE HIS DEATH... HE WANTED TO CALL IT *"DOJO 2000."*

THEY'RE QUITE *EXCEPTIONAL!* MY HUSBAND WAS A MASTER OF MOVEMENT AND ACTION!

DO YOU WANT TO SEE?

SURE, WHY NOT?

KYI!

HAN!

HAN!

WAAAH!!

CLAP CLAP

ZIING

ZIING

?

SSSSHH

DOJO

SO, DID YOU LIKE IT?

CLAP CLAP

MADAME KOKONINO, I NEED TO EXPLAIN SOMETHING TO YOU...

EVERY NIGHT FOR A YEAR, I'VE HAD NIGHTMARES ABOUT YOU! *EVERY NIGHT!*

RED ANTS, CROCODILES, ROLLER COASTERS, I KNOW THEM ALL!

THE ONLY THING I'M REALLY AFRAID OF HERE IS YOU...

...EVEN IF YOU WERE STANDING NEXT TO THE DEVIL HIMSELF!!

83

TAKE THE PRISONER DOWN!

IS THAT TRUE, MR. VARÈSE? YOU'VE *DREAMT* OF ME EVERY NIGHT FOR A YEAR?

I DIDN'T SAY *DREAMT*, I WAS TALKING ABOUT *NIGHTMARES!*

LISTEN, I THINK FENG DING WOULD LOVE A NEW FACE AT DINNER...

PROMISE ME YOU WON'T MENTION OUR LITTLE *DISAGREEMENTS,* AND I'LL RELEASE YOU UNCONDITIONALLY AFTER DESSERT...

WHAT DO YOU SAY?

THAT YOU JUST COMMUTED MY DEATH SENTENCE INTO A SOCIAL OBLIGATION. YOU WOULDN'T SEE THAT IN KANTOUCHA!

IN KANTOUCHA?

OF COURSE! DON'T YOU REMEMBER... THE LAST TIME YOU TRIED TO KILL ME! THE PACKAGE OF HEROINE YOUR SECRETARY SLIPPED INTO MY CAMERA!

?

BON APPÉTIT, EVERYONE!

34

THANK YOU, KYI. YOU MAY SERVE!

CAREFUL! THE SOUP IS HOT!

DZZZiii KSHH

PFFFFFF

?
?
?

NAPPIER!!! WHAT HAVE YOU DONE?!

IT... IT'S A KAKUZAKI 3000! HOW IS THAT *POSSIBLE?*

A ROBOT?!

!

BLAM

WOOM!

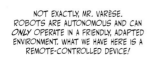

NOT EXACTLY, MR. VARÈSE. ROBOTS ARE AUTONOMOUS AND CAN *ONLY* OPERATE IN A FRIENDLY, ADAPTED ENVIRONMENT. WHAT WE HAVE HERE IS A REMOTE-CONTROLLED DEVICE!

HIS CONTROLLER SEES THROUGH HIS EYES AND MOVES HIM BY REMOTE CONTROL LIKE A PUPPETEER... AND HE'D HAVE TO BE A *DAMN GOOD* PUPPETEER TO FOOL ME!

WHAT'S THE POINT OF TELLING HIM ALL THIS?

HE WAS PART OF THE TEAM THAT MADE THE SWITCH IN THE MUSEUM! ... THIS TIME YOU'RE *GOING* TO TALK, VARÈSE!

NO! LET HIM GO! NAPPIER, LEAVE THIS ROOM IMMEDIATELY!

WHAT? BUT...

NAPPIER! OUT!

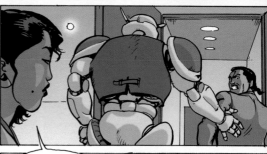

YOU MAY LEAVE ME ALONE WITH MR. VARÈSE, KYI.

YES, MA'AM.

MR. VARÈSE, I *BEG* YOU TO ANSWER ME! IS MY HUSBAND ALIVE?

GENERAL SYSTEM OVERRIDE

WE'RE TAKING KOKONINO WORLD! YES! *IMMEDIATELY!*

WE NO LONGER HAVE ANY *CHOICE!*

ALIVE? WHAT DO I KNOW?! I THOUGHT HE WAS KILLED FOUR YEARS AGO IN A PLANE CRASH!

I HAVE NO INFORMATION ON HIM! *I SWEAR IT!* I DON'T EVEN KNOW WHAT HE LOOKED LIKE...

HE LOOKED LIKE THIS, MR. VARÈSE. THIS IS ONE OF THE FEW PHOTOS WE HAVE OF HIM!

EXCUSE ME IF I DON'T TALK ABOUT IT. IT'S VERY HARD FOR ME TO LOOK AT!

MADAME KOKONINO? YOU'RE RIGHT, YOUR HUSBAND *IS* ALIVE!

HE RUNS A MARTIAN ARTS, I MEAN MARTIAL ARTS SCHOOL IN THE LITTLE TEMPLE ON THE MOUNTAIN ACROSS THE WAY!

HE IS ALIVE AND IN GOOD HEALTH. THE LAST TIME I SAW HIM, HE WAS JUMPING LIKE A MADMAN OVER MY CAR, FOLLOWED BY HIS TEAM OF SMURFS!

WHAT DID YOU SAY, MR. VARÈSE?

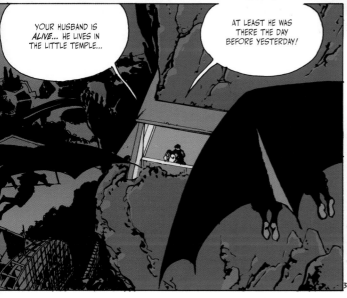

YOUR HUSBAND IS *ALIVE...* HE LIVES IN THE LITTLE TEMPLE...

AT LEAST HE WAS THERE THE DAY BEFORE YESTERDAY!

GOD HAVE MERCY ON ME, MR. VARÈSE! *FORGIVE* MY SINS AND MY MISTAKES!

OH!?

THE TELE-NINJAS!

KRA-DZIINK

OOOW

FOLLOW ME, VARÈSE, *QUICK!*

ZSSSSH!

OH SHIT!

ZOUP

THIS ELEVATOR WILL TAKE US DOWN TO THE CONTROL ROOM!

VNNNNN

FIOUU

HERE WE ARE... OH!

KIMAKO! WHAT A *PLEASANT* SURPRISE!

NAPPIER?!

!

HMM! FORGET THAT NAME, DARLING! MY NINJAS CALL ME "*WHITE SWORD*"!

38

AND BELIEVE ME, AFTER OPERATION "KOKONINO BAY," THAT NAME WILL BE ON EVERYONE'S LIPS! I'VE BEEN PREPARING FOR THIS MOMENT FOR FIVE YEARS! HA! HA! HOW DO YOU LIKE MY OUTFIT?

CAN WE BOTH GET IN THERE?

IT'LL BE A SQUEEZE!

DON'T TAKE YOUR EYES OFF THEM!

IT'S A TEN-MINUTE TRIP...

AAAH!

MADAME KOKONINO... *MONSTERS!* THERE ARE MONSTERS EVERYWHERE!

CALM DOWN, OLIVER! WE'RE GOING THROUGH A PARK ATTRACTION, THAT'S ALL!

HOW LONG TO LOAD THE TRUCKS?

ONE HOUR!

DON'T DRAG YOUR FEET! WE'LL MEET AT HQ!

DAMN! THEY'RE GOING UP TOWARD THE LITTLE TEMPLE!

VROM

FOLLOW THEM!

YES! SHE'S STILL A DAMN GOOD WOMAN, MY DEAR KIMAKO!

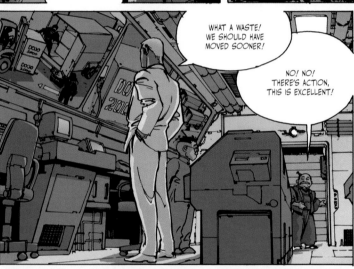

WHAT A WASTE! WE SHOULD HAVE MOVED SOONER!

NO! NO! THERE'S ACTION, THIS IS EXCELLENT!

COME ON! I'M ANXIOUS TO SEE MY ADORABLE WIFE!

KIMAKO!

TOKI!

SO IT WAS TRUE!

YOU'RE ALIVE!

LOOK OUT!

HERE, MASTER!

WHO'S BEEN HIT! WHERE IS FENG DING?

THE MAN WHO WOULD HAVE OPENED THE GATES TO *ETERNITY!*

THE MAN WHO WAS GOING TO MAKE US ALL IMMORTAL!

WILL I EVER BE FORGIVEN FOR ALL THE EVIL I'VE CAUSED? CAN YOU FORGIVE MY FAULTS AND MY MISTAKES, TOKI?

KIMAKO, THIS DISASTER IS ALL MY FAULT! MY LACK OF JUDGMENT IS *UNFORGIVABLE!*

I LOVED PLAYING GOD SO MUCH, FROM THE HEIGHTS OF MY OBSERVATORY... WATCHING THE INTRIGUES UNRAVEL IN THE WORLD I CREATED...

A *SACRIFICE* IS CALLED FOR!

GO HOME, CHILDREN, THE MASTER OF KOKONINO BAY WILL TEACH NO MORE...

WELL, YOU'RE NOT GOING TO LET HIM COMMIT *HARA-KIRI,* ARE YOU?

THE NEXT DAY AT DAWN...

NO *REGRETS*, MR. KOKONINO?

MANY, MR. VARÈSE.

WHAT HAVE I DONE WITH MY LIFE AND MY TALENT? COMPARED TO A MAN LIKE FENG DING... NOTHING AT ALL!

COME ON, DON'T BE SO *HARD* ON YOURSELF! YOU MUST HAVE PLANS...

THE SCENT OF MAGNOLIA
Art by Enrico Marini, story by Pop

HELLO!

DID YOU FIND SOMETHING?

...AND HAS THE DAY BEEN *PRODUCTIVE* FOR YOU?

YOU *SURPRISED* ME...

MAYBE. I'VE LOCATED *SEVERAL* INTERESTING SITES AND I'VE TAKEN SOME PICTURES.

NOT BAD. BUT *NOTHING* THAT COULD COMPARE TO LAST MONTH'S DISCOVERY.

HAVE YOU SENT YOUR REPORT TO THE *UNIVERSITY* YET?

NO. ...THE ANALYSIS WE MADE HERE IS TOO BASIC. I'VE CONTACTED SOME SPECIALISTS FOR A CORROBORATING EVALUATION...

ARE YOU SPENDING THE NIGHT HERE?

NO. I'M SPLITTING TO FEERNWOOD.

THE HOTEL IS MORE COMFORTABLE. ALSO, I WANT TO HAVE THE PICTURES DEVELOPED...

...AND THE SUPPLIES ARE GETTING LOW ANYWAY.

I'LL ENTRUST YOU WITH OUR FIND THEN. YOU CAN SEND IT TO MY LAB.

TAKE GOOD CARE OF IT.

DON'T WORRY.

BYE, BYE DADDY.

WRAK

WHAT THE...?

KA-POW KA-POW

100

THERE HE IS.

NOW BOARDING FOR MORGES AND LAUSANNE!

?!

EXCUSE ME PLEASE, YOUNG MAN....

I'M DOCTOR ELSWORTH... THE ONE WHO CONTACTED YOU...

OH, IT WAS YOU...

I HOPE YOU ENJOYED THE CRUISE.

WHATEVER. I LOST MY TASTE FOR THESE LAKE CRUISES LONG AGO...

NO, THANK YOU.

...PLUS, I *DIDN'T* SLEEP TOO WELL. I HAD TO GET UP *EARLY* TO CATCH THIS *DAMN* BOAT IN GENEVA.

AREN'T YOU GOING TO ASK ME THE *REASON* FOR THIS *MYSTERIOUS* RENDEZVOUS?

NO. BUT YOU'RE GOING TO TELL ME...

I'LL BE DIRECT: I INTEND TO GIVE YOU AN *EXCLUSIVE* PIECE OF INFORMATION.

PAY *ATTENTION.* I HAVE EXCELLENT *REASONS* TO BE PRUDENT. I *DEMAND* TOTAL DISCRETION UNTIL YOUR ARTICLE IS PUBLISHED.

WHOA. NOT SO FAST. FIRST, WHAT IS THIS *ABOUT,* DOCTOR?

IT'S ABOUT A SCIENTIFIC DISCOVERY... AND MORE.

BUT I'M A REPORTER, *NOT* A SCIENTIFIC COLUMNIST. *WHY* ME?

Zip

HE'S LATE.
I KNEW IT.

...THAT'S
HER.

WHAT THE...?

CRAP!!
I *FORGOT* TO
SET THE
ALARM!

SHIT...SHIT... SHIT!

CLAP CLAP CLAP

VRR-VRR-VRR-VRR

PIECE OF CRAP. OUT OF GAS!

AHHH! ANOTHER RED LIGHT.

RELAX. THERE'S THE BOTANIC GARDEN....

KEEP THE CHANGE...THANKS.

HALF AN HOUR LATE... SO MUCH FOR PUNCTUALITY.

MPF!

CLAC

HELLOOO. ANYBODY HERE...?!

SHE'S GONE.

109

THESE ARE *KATE'S* GLASSES...

YES. I RECOGNIZE THEM...

HOW IS THIS *POSSIBLE*...? SHE CAN'T SEE A *THING* WITHOUT HER GLASSES.

...WHAT WOULD SHE BE DOING AT THE LIBRARY *WITHOUT* HER GLASSES?

IS THERE ANY WAY OUT OF THE GARDEN NEAR HERE?

NO. ...UH. I DON'T THINK SO...

WAIT, NOW THAT I *THINK* OF IT...

COME ON. I WANT TO *SHOW* YOU SOMETHING...

HERE. IT'S SOME SORT OF...*SECRET* PASSAGE...

EVERYONE PRETTY MUCH *IGNORES* THE PASSAGE....

CHECK IT OUT. THE CHAIN HAS BEEN *FORCED.*

FOOTPRINTS. *SOMEONE* WENT THROUGH HERE RECENTLY.

MY GOD. *OH MY GOD.* YOU...YOU THINK SHE'S BEEN...

KIDNAPPED? I DON'T KNOW. MAYBE...

WHERE DOES THIS PATH LEAD?

TO THE PALACE OF NATIONS. BUT THE PASSAGE WAS BLOCKED OFF OVER FORTY YEARS AGO.

ALL RIGHT. I'LL CHECK THE OTHER SIDE...

IF YOU DON'T FIND HER IN THE LIBRARY, *CALL THE COPS.*

YES, MR. MALMSEY... SHE'LL TALK. SHE'S TERRIFIED.

I WANT THE ITEM *NOW!* I CAN'T BELIEVE IT TOOK YOU OVER A *YEAR* TO FIND THE GIRL!

DON'T WORRY. YOU'LL GET IT...

HEY, *YOU! WHERE* ARE YOU COMING FROM? THAT AREA'S *OFF LIMITS!*

RELAX, GRANDPA, I'M A REPORTER...

...ACCREDITED TO THE U.N.

GOOD FOR YOU...BUT THAT STILL DOESN'T *AUTHORIZE* YOU TO PASS THROUGH HERE.

YOUR PRESS I.D. DOESN'T GIVE YOU *UNLIMITED* ACCESS, YOU KNOW. I ALREADY TOLD ONE OF YOUR *COLLEAGUES* THE OTHER DAY...

WHAT? WHAT COLLEAGUE...?

UHM...AN AMERICAN I THINK. A BIG GUY WITH A RED CAP.

HE WAS WANDERING AROUND HERE, *CLAIMING* TO BE SCOUTING FOR A REPORT.

WEIRD. WHO COULD IT HAVE BEEN?

WELL, IF IT ISN'T THE AMAZON FROM THE BOAT...

UH OH. SHE *RECOGNIZED* ME...

I CAN'T GET *AWAY* FROM THAT WHALE.

VARÈSE, YOU *HANDSOME* DEVIL!

WHAT A *NICE* SURPRISE!

MMMH...

114

WHOA... THAT'S ONE HOT WELCOME.

THAT'S BECAUSE WE HAVEN'T *SEEN* YOU HERE IN SUCH A *LONG* TIME. WHAT'S THE *OCCASION?*

I'M LOOKING FOR A GUY...A REPORTER.

YOU'RE INTERESTED IN *MEN* NOW?

CUT IT OUT, SARI. I'M SERIOUS.

HE'S AMERICAN, A BIG GUY. HE WEARS A RED CAP...

YEAH, I KNOW THE GUY. HIS NAME IS POLLACK. ...CARL POLLACK.

THAT'S HIS OFFICE. HE'S A *STRANGE* GUY...

HE CLAIMS TO BE WORKING FOR A *SCIENTIFIC JOURNAL* BUT NOBODY'S EVER SEEN HIM WRITE AN ARTICLE...

...NOT ONCE. HE *ONLY* COMES HERE TO MAKE PHONE CALLS. AND HE *NEVER* TAKES OFF HIS CAP.

FRAGILE

...IT'S LIKE AN OBSESSION. *HEY! OLIVER!* YOU *CAN'T* JUST...WHAT DO YOU THINK YOU'RE *DOING?*

NONE OF YOUR BUSINESS, SWEETHEART. JUST LOOK THE OTHER WAY...

NOTHING...

WHEW.

AH...THE LAST PAGE ISN'T TOTALLY TORN OFF...

E GENEVA
FRIENDS
HÔNE

THE LAST WORD *HAS TO BE* RHÔNE. ...FRIENDS ...FRIENDS OF THE RHÔNE?

SARI. HAND ME THE PHONE BOOK.

...FRIENDS OF STUDENTS ...FRIENDS OF THE MOUNTAINS ...FRIENDS OF NATURE...OF RADIO. NO, *NOTHING* ON THE RHÔNE...

WHAT ARE YOU LOOKING FOR?

...THERE MUST BE A CONNECTION TO THE RHÔNE.

?!?

YOU'RE A DOLL. BYE SWEETIE, I'M OUT OF HERE...

UH ...BYE.

THAT WAS OLIVER VARÈSE! IS HE AS CRAZY AS EVER?

117

I KNOW WHAT YOU'RE LOOKING FOR.

GREAT. NOW I DON'T HAVE TO *WASTE* MY TIME.

YOU'RE *AMERICAN.*

YOU'RE THE ONE WHO *KILLED* MY FATHER! IT WAS *YOU!*

ANSWER ME! *ASSASSIN.* ...MPF...

YOU CARE ABOUT YOUR PRETTY FACE, DON'T YOU?

WHAT A WONDERFUL COINCIDENCE.

?!!

~MMPF

GEREON IS *SLEEPING* AT THE HOTEL. COME ON, LET'S GO FOR A *WALK*...

NO. NO. I'M IN A *HURRY* ...LET ME GO.

MOUETTES GENEVOISES
NAVIGATION
YACHT ELMA

HA. HA. NICE *PIECE*, EH?

SHE'S LIKE GLUE...

WHICH BOAT SAILS ON THE RHÔNE?

22

NONE OF THESE, BUDDY. BOARDING FOR THE RHÔNE IS AT THE BRIDGE ...IT'S A HIKE ...*BUMMER*, HUH?

ARE YOU *KIDDING* ME?!

ALL RIGHT, *RELAX.* WE'LL TAKE MY CAR THERE. I'VE *NEVER* LEFT A CUSTOMER HANGING...

MY NAME IS ARMAND CHARTER ...BUT EVERYONE JUST CALLS ME CHARTER. ARE YOU A TOURIST?

NOT REALLY. NO, I'M A REPORTER. OLIVER VARÈSE ...PLEASED TO MEET YOU.

A REPORTER? SHOULD HAVE TOLD ME. MY TREAT.

HERE WE ARE.

YOU KNOW THE RHÔNE *WELL,* MR. CHARTER?

LIKE THE BACK OF MY HAND.

THE *"FRIENDS"* OF THE RHÔNE," DOES THAT RING A BELL?

HMM...NO. WHO ARE THEY? *ECOLOGISTS?*

23

IT'S HOT. YOU SHOULD TAKE OFF YOUR JACKET OR YOU'LL FRY.

ALL ABOARD!

AAHHH! LOOK...

HUH?

A GIRL. SHE JUST JUMPED OFF THE BRIDGE.

DAMN. YOU'VE GOT TO CALM DOWN. IT'S JUST SOME KIDS WHO JUMPED IN TO SWIM...

...THEY DO IT EVERY SUMMER. YOU SCARED THE HELL OUT OF ME.

SORRY. I ...I'M A LITTLE HIGH-STRUNG.

SHE TALKED MR. MALMSEY.

24

VERY GOOD. AS SOON AS THE OBJECT IS IN A SECURE PLACE, YOU'LL DISPOSE OF HER.

NOW PAY ATTENTION. BE MORE CAREFUL THAN YOU WERE WITH HER FATHER... UNDERSTAND?

YES. SHE'LL DISAPPEAR WITHOUT A TRACE.

121

I'M VERY SORRY TO HAVE AWAKENED YOU, MR. PRESIDENT.

BUT I WANTED TO TELL YOU THAT EVERYTHING IS UNFOLDING ACCORDING TO YOUR PLAN...

YOU DID WELL, DEAR JASON.

I SHALL NOT *FORGET* YOUR DEVOTION.

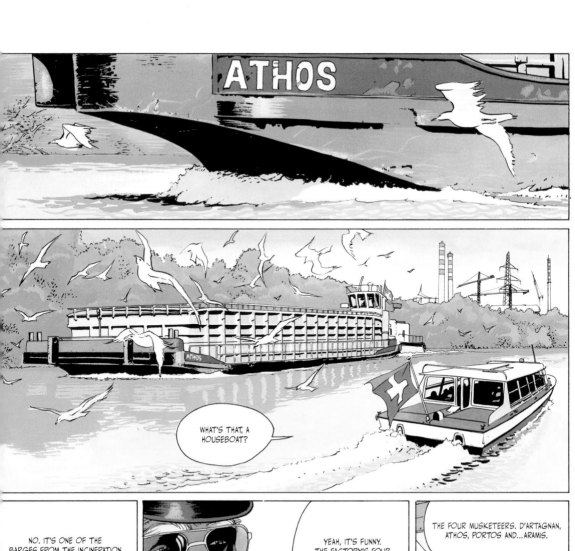

WHAT'S THAT, A HOUSEBOAT?

NO. IT'S ONE OF THE BARGES FROM THE INCINERATION FACTORY DOWNRIVER. IT'S FILLING UP ON GARBAGE IN GENEVA...

YEAH, IT'S FUNNY. THE FACTORY'S FOUR BARGES ARE NAMED AFTER DUMAS' MUSKETEERS...

THE FOUR MUSKETEERS. D'ARTAGNAN, ATHOS, PORTOS AND...ARAMIS.

ATHOS. STRANGE NAME FOR A BARGE...

AND THE TUGBOAT'S NAME IS TRÉVILLE, JUST LIKE THEIR BOSS.

AR...AMIS.

WHERE ARE THE *OTHER* BARGES?

PROBABLY AT THE FACTORY ...THE WHARF IS RIGHT IN FRONT OF US. WE'LL BE THERE IN FIVE MINUTES.

...FROM GENEVA ...ARAMIS ...RHÔNE...

SHE'S SOMEWHERE IN THAT FACTORY ...I'M *SURE* OF IT.

CAN I CALL THE POLICE WITH THE ON-BOARD RADIO?

HUH? THE COPS? *SURE* YOU CAN. BUT WHY THE *HELL* WOULD YOU?

I'LL EXPLAIN LATER...

IT'S NOTHING MORE THAN A *HUNCH*. IF I'M WRONG I'LL *NEVER* HEAR THE END OF IT....

THIS GUY'S NOT PLAYING WITH A FULL DECK.

LOOK, I'M NOT ASKING YOU TO *STORM* THE PLACE. JUST CHECK IT OUT. IT'S NOT *ROCKET* SCIENCE...

IT'S NOT AS EASY AS YOU THINK, MR. VARÈSE.

O.K. LET'S ROLL. WE'VE GOT A GREEN LIGHT.

I'LL GO WITH YOU... I KNOW THAT FACTORY BETTER THAN THESE COPS.

FULL STEAM *AHEAD* BOYS...

...CONTINUE STRAIGHT AND THEN TURN LEFT.

THERE'S ANOTHER ACCESS POINT THAT WAY ...BUT STOP AND TURN OFF THE SIREN FIRST...

126

WHAT?!

BASTARDS!
I'LL BLOW THEM ALL AWAY!

DON'T BE AN IDIOT, LEON! LET'S GET OUT OF HERE...

HEY ASSHOLES! EAT LEAD!

...TAKE COVER!!

HURRY!

WE'RE UNDER FIRE FROM AN AUTOMATIC WEAPON!

HEY!

STOP!

VVR

JOOARR

SKRIIII

SHIT! THAT BASTARD'S MAKING A RUN FOR IT!

YOU'LL BE *OKAY*, THE BULLET STOPPED IN YOUR THIGH.

THAT REPORTER'S GOT A GOOD NOSE FOR ACTION!

KATE!

GOOD GOD, KATE!

WIIOOOOOO

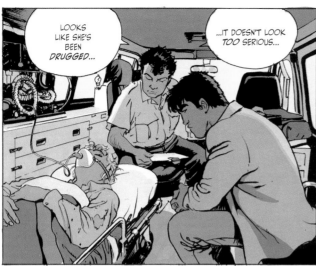

LOOKS LIKE SHE'S BEEN *DRUGGED*...

...IT DOESN'T LOOK *TOO* SERIOUS...

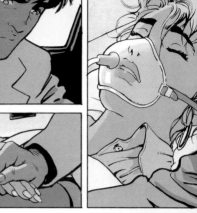

POLLACK WAS PLANNING TO *KILL* HER. *THAT'S* WHY THEY WERE HIDING OUT NEAR THE *FACTORY!*...

...AFTER *KILLING* HER, THEY WERE GOING TO *BURN* THE BODY IN THE INCINERATOR...

GULP!

BUT THERE WAS A *PROBLEM*... THE *FACTORY* RUNS 24 HOURS A DAY!

HMM?

YEAH. NO WAY IN WITHOUT BEING *CAUGHT*...

SO POLLACK FIGURED HE'D *THROW* THE BODY ONTO ONE OF THE *TRASH-BARGES*...

VILLE DE GENEVE
JARDIN BOTANIQUE
OUVERT
7H00 A 19H30

NEAR THE FACTORY THE BARGES FOLLOW A CHANNEL WHERE THEY'RE LEFT *WITHOUT* ANY SURVEILLANCE...

RIGHT AFTER THAT, THEIR LOAD GETS *BURNED!*

HOW *HORRIBLE!*

THAT'S WHY HE TOOK NOTES ON THE ROTATIONS OF THE *"MUSKETEERS"*... THEIR DEPARTURE FROM GENEVA, THEIR ITINERARY ON THE RHÔNE. THEIR ARRIVAL!

34

HOW DID THEY GET INTO THE AREA *UNNOTICED?*

THERE'S CONSTRUCTION GOING ON. THEY *MINGLED* WITH THE WORKERS...

DON'T MOVE, *ASSHOLE!*

35

DAMMIT!

OH JESUS!

OUT OF THE WAY!

HEY!

WHAT THE HELL? YOU ASSHOLE!

BY NOW POLLACK MUST HAVE FOUND WHAT HE WAS LOOKING FOR AND SPLIT...WELL?!

WHAT WAS HE LOOKING FOR?

THAT HAT! IT'S POLLACK!

STOP THAT MAN!

SHIT! THE REPORTER!

WHAT DO YOU *THINK* YOU'RE *DOING?*

HUH?

YOU *JERK!*

RAK

CHAF

AH!

LEAVE HIM...

...ALONE!

CHAK

HMM!

...

ARE YOU *OKAY,* HONEY?

YEAH! *THANK YOU,* WHAL... UHM MA'AM!

JESUS! *MOBY DICK* FELL ON MY HEAD!

?!

DID HE *HURT* YOU?

MY LITTLE *SWEETIE-PIE!*

HEY! AAAH! ENOUGH... I'M *SUFFOCATING!* MMMPF...

CLIC!

CALIFORNIA, UNITED STATES, A FEW DAYS LATER...

...FBI? WHAT DO *YOU* WANT?

TO SPEAK WITH DR. MALMSEY!

HIS OFFICE IS IN THE TOWER. I'LL TELL HIM YOU'RE HERE...

40

IT'S *GIGANTIC!*

...YEAH!

IT'S A REAL *MIRACLE* OF LIFE!

YES! WE WERE *LUCKY* TO FIND YOU *ALIVE!*

I WASN'T *TALKING* ABOUT MYSELF. I MEANT THE *LEAF*...

OH! RIGHT! ...THE LEAF ...IT'S *VERY RARE*...!

NO, OLIVER! IT'S *UNIQUE!* WHEN WE FOUND IT, IT HAD JUST *DIED*... 20 MILLION YEARS BEFORE!

I HAVE *NO IDEA* WHAT THAT MEANS...

LET ME *EXPLAIN!* THE LEAF WAS SEALED IN CLAY, *SAFE* FROM OXYGEN...

ALL THE CELL STRUCTURES WERE *MIRACULOUSLY* INTACT... AS IF IT HAD *JUST* FALLEN OFF ITS STEM...

COME ON! I WANT TO SHOW YOU SOMETHING...

ARE YOU THE FBI AGENTS?

...DR. MALMSEY ISN'T HERE...

WHAT?

...BUT HE'S BEEN *INFORMED* OF YOUR PRESENCE. HE'S *EXPECTING* YOU ON THE HIGH TERRACE! IT'S AT THE *TOP* OF THE TOWER!

YOU TAKE THE *EXTERIOR* ELEVATOR...

TO THE *TOP*...?

138

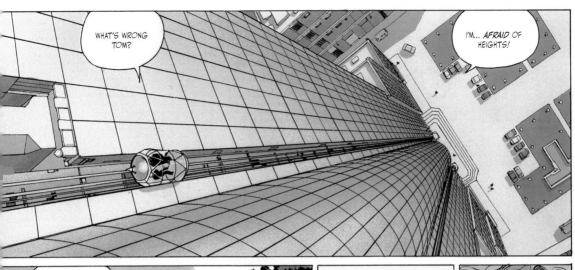

42

YOU SEE, THERE ARE *MANY* SIMILARITIES AND DIFFERENCES BETWEEN A PRESENT DAY MAGNOLIA AND THE OLDER ONE ...

WE THEN INTRODUCED THEM INTO THE NUCLEUS OF A *PRESENT* MAGNOLIA CELL, WHICH IN TURN PASSED THE *DIFFERENCES* ON TO ITS OFFSPRING...

CLIC

CLIC

THIS WAY WE GREW NEW MAGNOLIAS, WHICH HAD MOST OF THE *CHARACTERISTICS* OF THE ANCIENT ONE: THE FORM OF THE LEAVES, THE SCENT AND THE COLOR OF THE FLOWERS...

THAT'S *INCREDIBLE!*

SO, IT WAS ENOUGH TO TAKE SOME SEQUENCES OF DNA FROM THE LEAF... *AMONG THEM,* THE ONES THAT *CREATE* THOSE DIFFERENCES.

WOUR WOUR WOUF

THAT *NOISE!* SOUNDS LIKE A...

HMPF...

SON OF A *BITCH!* MALMSEY IS *ESCAPING!*

BYE BYE! *MORONS!*

HELLO GENTLEMEN! I WAS *EXPECTING* YOU...I'M DR. THEODORE K. MALMSEY!

?!?

YOU?! THEN WHO'S IN THE CHOPPER?

MY ASSISTANT, WHY?

FOLLOW ME, WE'LL BE MORE *COMFORTABLE* IN THE GREENHOUSE...

HERE I'VE GATHERED THE *RAREST* PLANTS, THE MOST *BEAUTIFUL* FLOWERS, THE MOST *DELICATE* FLORAL SCENTS...

...IT'S A UNIQUE COLLECTION, ALL *MODESTY* ASIDE!

DR. MALMSEY! WE HAVE SOME *QUESTIONS* TO ASK YOU REGARDING THE *DEATH* OF DR. ELSWORTH!

QUITE... IMPRESSIVE!

IS IT *TRUE* THAT THE *PROFESSOR* GOT IN TOUCH WITH ONE OF YOUR LABS?

PSHiiT PSHiiT

PLEASE, GENTLEMEN! BE *SERIOUS!* I DON'T BOTHER MYSELF WITH THESE *TRIFLES*...

THIS MAN *CLAIMS* TO KNOW YOU. HE'S A HIRED *KILLER...* CARL POLLACK!

RIDICULOUS! I'VE NEVER SEEN HIM BEFORE...

CLEARLY, THIS MAN IS LYING...

SAY...YOUR BABY MAGNOLIAS... ARE THEY WORTH A LOT?

LIKE ALL *EXCEPTIONAL* THINGS!

UH HUH! THAT *EXPLAINS* YOUR RECENT TROUBLES!

YES! BUT THERE'S MORE...

MALMSEY IS A BIG *COLLECTOR* OF RARE PLANTS! ABOVE ALL, HE'S AN *EXPERT* PERFUME HUNTER...

PERFUME HUNTER?

HE CONTROLS A *VAST* EMPIRE: BIOCHEMISTRY, GENETICS, PHARMACEUTICALS... BUT HIS *GREATEST* INTEREST IS IN PERFUMES!

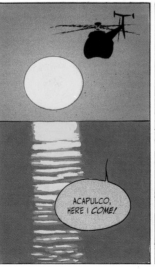

ACAPULCO, HERE I *COME!*

HIS EXPERTS TRAVEL THE WORLD IN SEARCH OF FLOWERS WITH *RARE* SCENTS... A *VERY* PROFITABLE ENTERPRISE! THE PERFUME INDUSTRY IS *BLOOMING!*

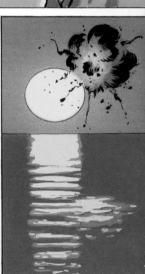

MORE THAN THE LEAF, IT'S THE *SCENT* OF A LOST FLOWER THAT MALMSEY WANTED...

HIS *UNCONTROLLABLE* DESIRE LED HIM TO *MURDER* MY FATHER. I'M SURE OF IT.

HE WILL BE SURPRISED THAT DESPITE OUR *MODEST* MEANS, WE WERE ABLE TO *RECREATE* THE PLANT HE WAS DREAMING ABOUT.

YOU KNOW, WE ALSO WORK WITH SCENT HUNTERS.

SOMETIMES THEY COME TO PICK UP *EXHALATIONS* OF OUR RARE PLANTS. THEY'LL BE *EAGER* TO SEE THE MAGNOLIAS BLOOM.

OLIVER! I OWE YOU A *PROPER* "THANK YOU"...

I DON'T KNOW WHAT YOUR MAGNOLIA *SMELLS* LIKE... BUT I'LL NEVER FORGET THE *TASTE* OF YOUR *GRATITUDE!*

46

THE END

IN 1991, A TEAM HEADED BY PROF. EDWARD GOLENBERG OF THE UNIVERSITY OF CALIFORNIA UNCOVERED A MAGNOLIA LEAF IN THE REGION OF CLARKIA (IDAHO, UNITED STATES), MIRACULOUSLY PRESERVED IN CLAY FOR 20 MILLION YEARS. INCREDULOUS AT FIRST, THE BIOLOGISTS ACCEPTED THE OBVIOUS: THE DNA OF THE LEAF WAS INTACT. IT'S THE OLDEST SAMPLE OF "LIVING MATERIAL" EVER DISCOVERED.